Voyage to the Moon

Written by Debbie-Ann Wylie

Illustrated by Dara Jordan-Brown

Published by Debbie-Ann Thompson-Wylie
Black Rock, Tobago,
Trinidad and Tobago, W.I.

Cover Design by Dara Jordan-Brown

ISBN 978-976-97281-0-3 (paperback)
ISBN 978-976-97281-1-0 (eBook)

To my energetic boys
who always keep me on my toes.
...be kind, be brave, be you.

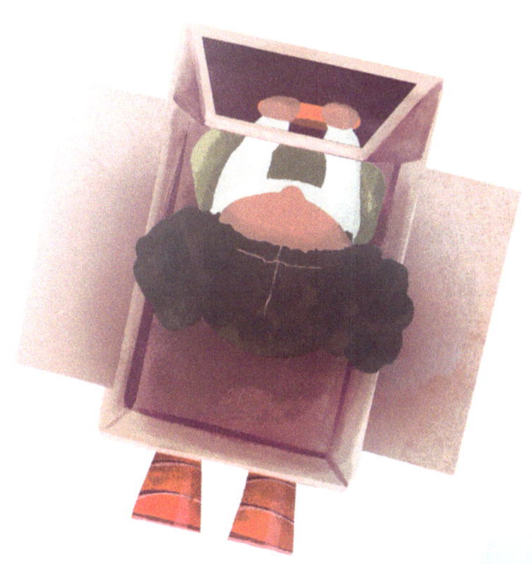

I'm on my voyage
to the moon.
Hooray!
I will see you soon.

It was my wish
since a bug,
to give the moon
a big, big hug.

I smile as I focus,
I feel proud.

I ascend and I zoom
past the cloud.

Next,
the atmosphere
I breach.

The moon is now within my reach.

You,
Stop!
Right over
there!
How dare you come so near!

Why aren't you
fearful of me?
What is it
do you really see?

Your face shining
so bright,
radiating the sky
at night.

Every crater,
giant and small,
those wounds, they
tell it all.

Hmmm

But how could you forget
about what has none seen yet?
Beware of what you do.

Remember,
I have a dark
side too.

Truthfully,
I was not aware.

I saw only your
glowing glare.

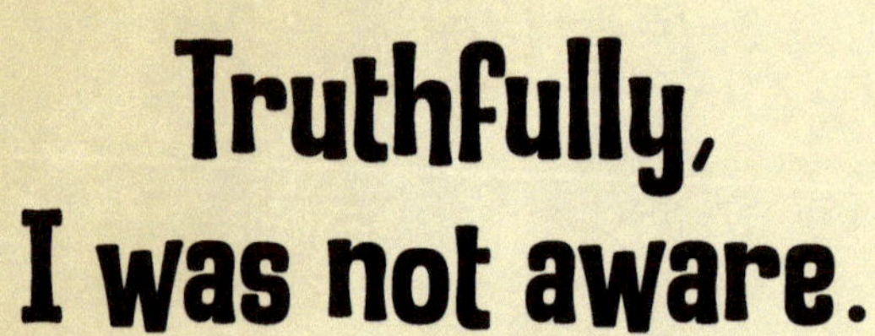

To me your alluring gaze
beckoned.
It's your silent call,
I so reckoned.

Be wary of touch, best to look.

These are rules in
my safety book.

Many threats
and unknown dangers
lurk around
mysterious strangers.

I thank you for giving insight

into my own pitiful plight.

I will take heed to what you say
and be cautious
in every way.

DID YOU KNOW?

Did you know that there is a dark side of the Moon?

The dark side of the Moon is the side of the Moon that always faces away from earth.
This side of the Moon cannot be seen from Earth.

The dark side of the Moon is sometimes called "the far side of the Moon".

The side of the Moon that is always faced towards Earth is called "the near side of the Moon". This is the side of the Moon that we can see from Earth.

WORD BANK

Isn't it fun to learn new words?
Here are a few words to add to your word bank.

<table>
<tr><td>Alluring</td><td>Beckoned</td><td>Breach</td></tr>
<tr><td>Glare</td><td>Insight</td><td>Plight</td></tr>
<tr><td></td><td>Voyage</td><td></td></tr>
</table>